MW00946294

FOR ALL THE
WONDERFUL PEOPLE
WHO CAN LAUGH,
SMILE, AND KEEP ON
KEEPIN' ON WHEN
TIMES GET TOUGH.

YOU WILL CHANGE
THE WORLD.

Copyright © 2020 by Jonathan C. Nordstrom

All rights reserved. No part of this publication may be reproduced, distributed or transmitted in any form or by any means, including photocopying, recording, or other electronic or mechanical methods, without the prior written per-mission of the publisher, except in the case of brief quotations embodied in critical reviews and certain other noncommercial uses permitted by copyright law. For permission requests, write to the publisher, addressed "Attention: Permissions Coordinator," at the address below.

The Omnibus Publishing

5422 Ebenezer Rd., PO Box 152

Baltimore, MD 21162

www.theomnibuspublishing.com

Publisher's Note: This is a work of fiction. Names, characters, places, and incidents are a product of the author's imagination. Locales and public names are sometimes used for atmospheric purposes. Any resemblance to actual people, living or dead, or to businesses, companies, events, institutions, or locales is completely coincidental.

Ordering Information: Special discounts are available on quantity purchases by corporations, associations, and others. For details, contact the publisher at the address above.

Baltimore / Jonathan C. Nordstrom — First Edition

ISBN 978-1-7335985-3-8 / Library of Congress Cataloging-In-Publication Data, Control Number Contact Publisher

Printed in the United States of America

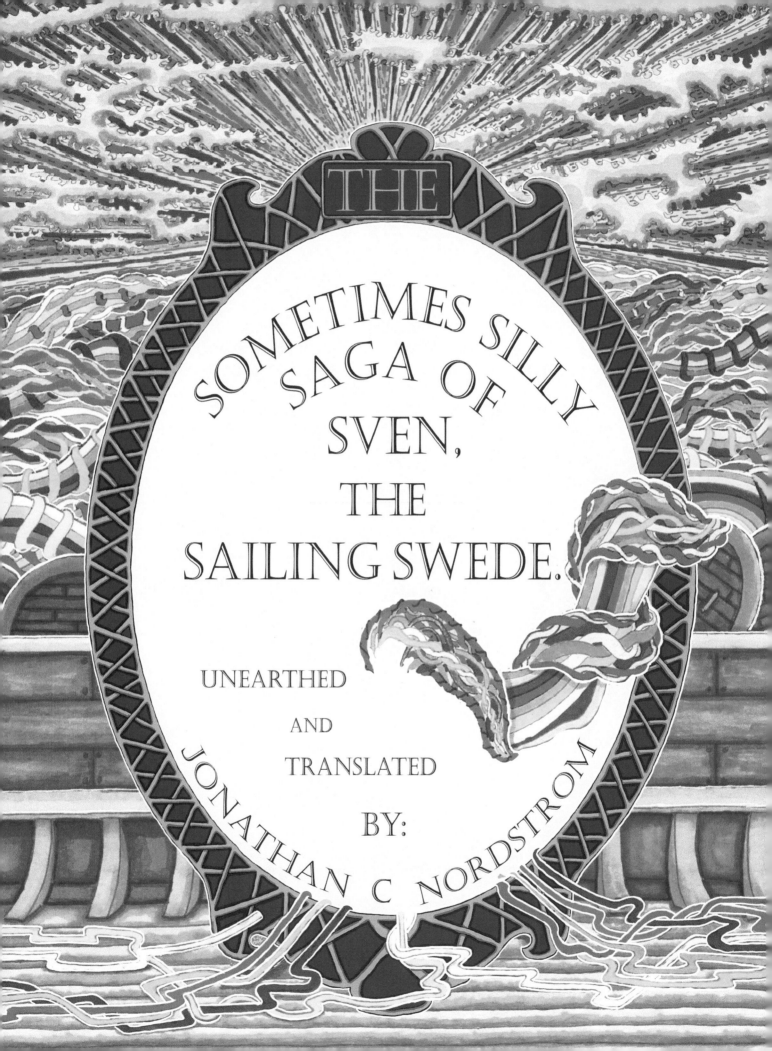

Please allow me to introduce myself,
I'm known as Sven the Sailing Swede.
I've crossed most waters around this world,
I'm a travelin' man, indeed.

I'm not one of those nasty old Vikings,
Who plundered all around the sea.
They are too hotheaded for my liking.
I choose to live peaceful and free.

The escapades I've been a part of,
Will doubtless make your toes curl!
Excitement will cause hair to stand up,
And force your eyeballs to whirl.

I'll share a glorious story with you,
Of animals never spied;
With exquisite, exotic locales.
I have no tales which I will hide.

Have you ever heard somebody mutter,
Take that tale with a grain of salt?
I am certain the first to voice that phrase,
And I don't see it as a fault.

A blue whale and I went on a long hike,
And when we were miles inland,
She began sobbing how she missed the sea,
A feeling that I understand.

I gave her a grain of salt from my stash,
Which she devoured with delight!
The salt immediately made her happy,
And thus the phrase was born that night.

Translator's Notes – Vikings roamed the sea from 793–1066 AD. If Sven was indeed around during the Viking era, he is well over 1,200 years old.

Pliny the elder is widely considered the source of the phrase, "Take with a grain of salt." He was a Roman author, born in AD 23, well before Sven's time. Sven may have been exaggerating his role in this phrase.

It's pretty much an impossibility that whales can walk.

Sagas are Scandinavian tales passed from generation to generation, mostly oral. Sven's saga is remarkably well preserved and even book-like with complete illustrations.

The first story to come from my travels,
Occurred right under my ship's hull.
As I sailed in the Caribbean Sea,
The breeze had slowed down to a lull.

Rowing through slack surf was taxing,
The action produced so much sweat.
Growing hot I slid into the water,
As by then I was soaking wet.

While I splashed and swam about,
A fantastic noise I did hear.
The lovely sound of an organ,
Full of music, bubbly and clear.

I dove down deeper to investigate
And to my utter disbelief,
I spied a beautiful coral organ,
Created from the incredible reef.

Settled snugly in front of this organ,
Sat a crimson cephalopod.
That is octopus to be specific,
And that sure did seem a bit odd.

She saw me staring intently at her,
While she gently tickled the keys.
The Beatles song, "Octopus's Garden,"
Sprung forth with a graceful ease.

Unfortunately, I ran out of breath!
I had to shoot up quick for air.
Desperately, I wanted to hear more,
But there just was no time to spare!

I took in a humongous gulp of air,
Descending with much haste I dove.
By the time I arrived she was long gone,
Along with the music she wove.

I swam to my ship and began to row,
My mood was quite bright and upbeat.
I was certain I'd find more amusements.
I'd search far and wide from my seat!

Translator's Notes - This section of his saga is quite waterlogged. But it is very clear that this is the beginning of his extensive wandering.

An octopus can be quite clever. But clever enough to play an organized composition on an organ?

Sound waves produced by an organ don't transmit clearly through water.

Which year did Sven discover this Octopus? The Beatles did not release the song, "Octopus's Garden," until 1969.

In the doldrums I lie without a breeze,
As no wind came to fill up my sails.
With nothing to do I sat and waited.
Alas, it was to no avail.

I soon grew very weary and bored,
And rowed towards the nearest shore.
The rowing felt like backbreaking labor,
But waiting on wind was a bore.

With my ship firmly ashore on dry land,
Something quite odd made me look twice.
Was that a rare sea unicorn on land?
I had to rub my eyes and look thrice.

She was having an incredible time,
Bending under a wooden pole.
I saw her smile and dance heartily,
To music filled with island soul.

She was a part of a massive party;
It appeared to be so much fun!
I simply wanted to have fun as well,
So I broke into a brisk run.

The very instant she spied me running,
She dove back into the sea.
I could not understand what I did wrong.
What's not to like about me?

Islanders welcomed me with laughter,
But when they saw that I was sad,
One gently said he knew why she left.
No one wanted me to feel bad.

They explained Sea Unicorns are shy,
And not very keen on strangers.
They have known her since she was a calf,
And as such, did not pose a danger.

Knowing all that made me feel much better.
We laughed and danced all through the night.
I waved good bye to them in the morning,
And my ship sailed off at first light.

* Translator's Notes – Wow! Where to begin? A Viking in the Caribbean?!

Due to the detailed illustration, Sven was talking about a narwhal...doing the limbo...on a warm sandy beach.

Once dubbed as the Unicorn of the Sea, Narwhals live throughout the Arctic. They are hardly a warm weather creature, let alone one who could walk ashore and bend under a pole.

Sven appears to have visited the Caribbean. The island originators of the limbo are Trinidad and Tobago. I could not distinguish the year he visited. Based on his previous visit with the octopus, I would guess the late 1960s? Remarkable!

On the water there was a strong breeze,
Sending me sailing East and North.
I soon saw a gorgeous new shoreline.
Along down this path I forged forth.

After exploring for some lovely weeks,
I reached the mouth of a great bay.
I decided I should go explore,
There is time to burn on this day.

There were oysters, fish, and waterfowl.
This part of my trip did not bore.
After a while this great bay narrowed,
Into a port named Baltimore.

I sailed my ship into the harbor,
Where the fun is I do not know.
An old sailor told me about races,
At a great place called Pimlico.

I skedaddled inland towards the racetrack,
And found the way to my seat.
Delighted, I watched the big race,
Which turned out to be a real treat.

On the track was an astonishing sight,
A blue crab rode a terrapin!
Quite small and engulfed by large horses,
Surely there was no way they'd win.

With a trumpet the starting gates opened
And out the contestants all dashed.
But the only team that captured my eye
Was a tiny blue and tan flash.

The race did not even seem close to fair,
The duo won by a mile.
I headed on back towards my longboat,
Shaking my head with a smile.

The blue crab and terrapin had taught me,
A lesson not soon forgotten.
Never judge a book by its cover,
Your judgment may well be rotten.

I boarded and rowed back into the bay,
Which the locals called the Chesapeake.
My ship sailed forth to my next adventure,
One hopefully just as unique.

Translator's Notes - Baltimore, Maryland was founded on July 30, 1729.

Pimlico racetrack opened October 25, 1870. This part of his journey could have happened between that date and today.

Northward the current carried me,
To a nice place known by Vikings.
L'Anse aux Meadows was the town name,
It's beauty was to my liking.

Sailing to Canada makes one hungry,
And I searched for a breakfast treat.
I sat in a diner and looked around,
I almost fell out of my seat.

In the kitchen was an amazing thing,
A beaver but with a duck bill!
He was most cheerful while flipping flapjacks,
And singing a song with a trill.

"Platy-cake, Platy-cake, webfoot can,
flip you a pancake, as fast as man!"

My order of flapjacks came piping hot,
They smelled incredibly fine.
I smothered them in sweet maple syrup,
And they truly tasted divine.

I devoured my meal in mere seconds,
Wiping syrup off of my chin.
I still could not believe what I had seen,
My mouth still holding a huge grin.

Belly full, I waddled to my ship,
Thinking of what next I should do.
I felt a strong breeze blow in from the East,
And right then I most certainly knew.

I'd travel down this tremendous river,
Known to go from sea to great lakes.
There would be so many great things to see!
Going west would be no mistake.

Once again my beloved sail billowed,
Sending me out far from the shore.
If there's one thing I know for certain,
It's my journeys are never a bore.

*Translator's Notes - L'anse aux Meadows, a place known to be the first landing spot for Vikings in North America on the island of Newfoundland in Canada, around AD 1000. For Sven to say his friends vacationed there makes him very old indeed.

On that note - There was no stainless steel kitchen equipment in AD 1000.

One more note – I'm pretty sure the picture is of a platypus, a species that lives in the warm weather climate of eastern Australia. Newfoundland is a bit far out of their range.

Last note - Platypus have a duck like bill, lay eggs, have a beaver like tail, and a venomous spur on their leg. I would not want one flipping my pancakes with all that fur & venom!*

Cruising through another sizable bay,
then down the length of a river.
I rowed through many contraptions called locks,
where to lakes I was delivered.

Those Great Lakes were as enormous as seas,
And I took in all the nice sights.
After some days I spied a grand hotel,
Much to my exhausted delight.

It was smack in the middle of summer,
With weather simply ideal.
When I strolled onto the hotel's great porch,
it's size appeared truly unreal.

I sat right down to enjoy the cool shade,
In a chair made wonderfully.
Looking around I saw something quite strange,
a sight I never thought to see.

An adorable fluffy ball of fur
With eyes as big as dinner plates,
Was gleefully devouring some fudge.
It sure looked like it tasted great!

Finishing her gooey, chocolate treat,
she burped and looked all around.
Then slowly walked off the great old porch
without making any sound.

I sat a while bemused and stunned,
Before shifting into a laugh.
It was the cutest thing I'd ever seen!
I was happy to have crossed paths.

Suddenly I felt a craving hit me
For one of those fudgy delights.
I bought a box and ate it all down,
Then smiling, turned in for the night.

I spent the long night in that grand hotel,
Waking with a stupendous yawn.
I brushed my teeth then braided my long hair,
And headed out again at dawn.

There was no limit of time I could spend
On these lakes that looked like seas.
Out I drifted with the slow moving current,
My mind peacefully at ease.

Translator's Notes – Sven must have stopped at the Grand Hotel on Mackinac Island, Michigan. Built in 1887, this hotel has the world's largest porch.

It appears the creature Sven saw was a slow Loris, indigenous to Southeast Asia. They are omnivores, but fudge does not appear to be a staple of their diet. How did yet another tropical animal end up this far north?

I had been adrift in the lakes for days,
And must have fallen deep asleep.
For I awoke in a vast stinky swamp,
With dank mud in which I'd not leap.

Lily pads and ferns crowded a great marsh,
Along with great rotting logs.
Sitting astride one to my great surprise,
Were gabbing and frolicking frogs.

They had zero worries in the world.
They heartily feasted on grubs.
Which turned out on closer inspection,
Was a sack of human toe nubs!

Without moving I looked down at my feet
And quickly counted my ten toes.
Exhaled an enormous sigh of relief,
Then I thought, *where DID they get those*?

I started to get extremely nervous.
More than nervous, I became scared!
To quietly leave the murky fen,
My ship I softly prepared.

I slowly paddled back out to the lake,
Let out a fresh sigh of relief;
Arrived at wonderful open water,
My mind was still in disbelief.

With a sudden start I awoke again,
In the Middle of the great lake.
Were talking frogs part of a crazy dream?
Was it a big dreamy mistake?

Awake or asleep I knew for certain,
Those wacky frogs I would not miss.
Heading my boat back out to the seaway,
I was back in a state of bliss.

Translator's Notes - Sven admits it may have been a dream. Could he have taken in too much sun and hallucinated?

Bullfrogs are common throughout the Great Lakes. He could have landed in a great swamp.

How he came up with frogs eating toadstools, er, toed stools, is beyond me. The term "toadstool" refers to how these mushrooms look like toads would enjoy sitting on them.

But, there were frogs not toads. Something punny is going on here!

East through the Seaway I swiftly passed,
America left in my wake.
Across the Atlantic Ocean I sailed,
With nary a glitch nor mistake.

I landed smoothly in the south of France,
After weeks being out at sea.
I decided to take an extended hike,
To set my land loving legs free.

Unsure where my journey should begin,
Leisurely to the North I strolled.
The country shone with intense beauty,
And my eyes soon saw mountains unfold.

There were so many dazzling visions!
I had wandered about for weeks.
I discovered myself in Switzerland,
And here is where things get unique.

Entering a magnificent valley,
I spotted something really neat.
'Twas a wrinkly, little, lime green lizard,
Walking about on his rear feet.

I was almost too astonished to speak,
But managed to croak out "Hello!"
He gave me a grin and said, "Kia ora!"
He was a nice little fellow.

We sat and chatted for quite a while.
I learned he was a tuatara.
He was on his own personal journey,
From a place that was quite a-far-ah.

After some hours we said farewell,
As I did not have much more time.
For I was heading towards the South,
His journey different from mine.

Lazily wandering back to the shore,
My mind felt as if in a trance.
I was mesmerized by the nice lizard
And I found myself back in France.

Climbing back into my trusty old ship,
I decided to head towards home.
I was growing a little bit weary,
The earth is a big place to roam.

Translator's Notes - Sven appears to have hiked the French and Swiss Alps.

Native to New Zealand, tuatara lizards are not known in other places. They are rare and are actually not lizards. Its closest relatives lived around the time of dinosaurs! Tuataras are an endangered species in their native habitat.

To see a tuatara hiking on two feet, in the Alps, is quite fascinating indeed!

The Journey of a thousand miles begins with a single step.

Towards my homeland I set a new course,
Barreling on home with full sails.
A thought popped into my frazzled brain,
I'd need proof of my wondrous tales.

Right then I spied a very large island,
And veered in my vessel quite swift.
I needed to bring back a souvenir,
And maybe pick up my mom a nice gift.

I wanted something unique and perfect,
So up a river I did sail.
Continuing for a very long distance,
Until a large city I hailed.

Finally there stood a large factory,
The sign said, "Faraday Balloons."
Somehow the name struck me rather funny,
And I guffawed just like a loon.

There were many wonders in this building,
Including floating colored balls.
But those balls were not even the strangest.
What came next surely beats all.

From behind a box in the large warehouse,
I Heard quite a bubbly, "Hallo!"
Peering around the box I saw the source.
I hoped my surprise would not show.

If she saw the shock plainly on my face,
There was no sign of her concern.
A prickly thing that kept talking,
On vast balloon lore she was learned.

For well over an hour and a half,
She continued rambling on.
I finally got a word in edgewise,
And told her I had get gone.

She handed me strings of five balloons,
And said they were five for a pence.
What on earth that meant I did not know,
And embarrassed I grew sort of tense.

She saw my unease then giggled and said,
"It's a little British money.
But since you've been a wonderful listener,
Today the balloons are free, honey!"

I thanked her for her generosity,
Then gathered up all the great loot.
I was grateful for the amazing gift,
And towards home I began to scoot.

Translator's Notes - It's striking that Sven chose England to land. The first significant raid by Vikings in 793 AD was in Lindisfarne, England. The Vikings remained a scourge there for hundreds of years.

Michael Faraday invented rubber balloons in 1824 in London, England. Sven's account of balloons is shockingly accurate.

According to his picture, the saleswoman would have been an echidna. This presents many questions. They are indigenous to the warm climates of Australia and New Guinea. Her spines would likely have popped balloons and I'm astonished that she walked and talked.

The air grew colder as northward I sailed,

My beard grew salty and frozen.

Throughout the trip I felt so close to home,

And the land that I had chosen.

That night I pulled ashore with a light swish,

As it had been snowing for days.

The stunning northern lights were a-flicker,

And I was simply amazed.

The beauty of my country was surreal,

Sitting down I took in the view.

When out of the corner of my left eye,

I saw something that was askew.

There was an incredible bird singing

And dancing in the fresh snow!

I had been around Sweden my whole life

And of this bird I did not know.

Motionless I watched a gorgeous dance,

For hours it seemed to have lasted.

When finally it grew tired

And away into night he blasted.

I sat in wonder for a bit longer,

Still in awe of what I'd witnessed.

I remembered I was nearly at home,

Leapt and dashed off with a quickness.

My home appeared just beyond the next rise.

I was thrilled and filled with delight!

I had need of an evening of good rest,

After my long day and odd night.

When I happily burst through my doorway,

Once again there was a surprise.

I could not believe what awaited me,

I had to rub twice at my eyes!

Translator's Notes – We are starting to see a complete picture of Sven's life. Clues throughout his book refer to his hometown as a small municipality in southern Sweden.

If I had not seen the picture, I would have thought Sven saw was a bird late on its migratory route. This bird; however, is a rufous breasted kookaburra, native to Australia. The snow and cold would definitely not have made it dance and sing.

Sitting comfortably in my armchair,
With a fire all ablazin',
Unbelievably was a fish reading.
The whole mad scene was amazin'!

I stood with my jaw dropped wide open;
Slowly, he looked up from his book.
He bookmarked his place, smiled, and said,
"This is not as strange as it looks.

"I'm Humuhumunukunukuapua'a,
Or Hummy for short, if you please.
We have mutual friends that sent me,
If that helps put your mind at ease."

He described a familiar story,
Of wonders that I had observed.
How creatures worked hard to meet me,
For a story that must be heard.

It seems after I'd met the octopus,
A tale quickly spread and whirled,
That I could see in the secretive life,
Of the creatures of the world.

Sometimes silly stories stick and are told,
The animals could plainly see.
They went to unbelievable places,
Hoping to show it cannot be.

"We truly cannot live like we acted,
And we just want humans to know,
Our world is rapidly changing,
There's a shift in the ebb and flow.

Please think of wonders that may lie unseen,
and do your very best to care,
so that all the great future wanderers,
discover life everywhere."

I'll never forget the look on his face,
As he dashed out the front door.
There appeared to be much more unsaid,
While I stared blankly at the floor.

I stood and processed all he conveyed,
I felt I had much to say.
Making sure his words would not be lost,
I wrote down my tale the next day.

*Translator's Notes: It appears Hummy truly cared about this cause!

A humuhumunukunukuapua'a is a triggerfish. It's habitat is in the tropical waters of the Indo Pacific and it is the state fish of Hawaii. It would have swum over 7,000 miles to reach Sweden, through frigid and turbulent waters.

I would very much like to have an adventure as unique as Svens'. If we step up to become better stewards of the planet, journeys that are as amazing as his can continue! We likely won't see an octopus playing the piano; however, if we're lucky, maybe we'll get to see the wonderful octopus itself!

Sven left a final stanza in his book. It is, indeed, a fitting ending.

"My hope in life is that you all can see
With your own traveling eyes,
That marvels abound in this gorgeous world,
And the joy of unknown surprise!"

More Books by Jonathan C. Nordstrom

Sometimes Sleep

Mom's Choice Award Winner: Gold Honoree,
Gelett Burgess Award Winner, and Top 100 Notable Books
from Shelf Unbound.

A delightful journey through a beautiful dreamscape, filled
with lush images and loving poetry. Count sheep, rock on a
gentle wave, or ride a waterfall. Each image is richly
hand-drawn and paired with kid friendly poetry.

Hardcover: ISBN 9780986243769

Shimmer

Self-taught artist and break out children's book writer,
Jonathan C. Nordstrom, brings another incredible story to
life! Immerse yourself in the touching and hilarious
journey of a young droplet out on his first adventure!

Jonathan's incredible, hand drawn illustrations paired with
clever, kid friendly prose, will captivate and delight readers
of all ages.

Hardcover: ISBN 9780996675376

The Mouse at 61 House

Meet Mr. Jingles! He's a cheeky little mouse desperate
to join the brave fire fighting crew at nearby 61 House.
After moving in uninvited, things immediately begin to go
very wrong. While his intentions are good, his actions are
misunderstood and Mr. Jingles quickly becomes the fire
house nuisance. Then late one night disaster strikes! Can the
crew count on Mr. Jingles to help them save their beloved
firehouse?

Another spirited adventure brought to life by multi-award
winning author and illustrator, Jonathan C. Nordstrom, a
fireman from the actual 61 House in Virginia, USA.

Hardcover: ISBN 9780998681108

CPSIA information can be obtained
at www.ICGtesting.com
Printed in the USA
LVHW070147021020
667640LV00023BA/429